Tico the Astronomer

Written & Illustrated by

Deft Mutt

Tico, a coyote who lives in the forest, was walking around one day and found an empty can.

Oh No! His nose got stuck in it.

Getting rid of this can is not going to be easy, Tico
thought as he struggled to remove it.

But finally, the can flew off his nose. "Free at last!" Tico exclaimed, relieved to be rid of the can.

And the can landed over a bottle!

Tico was amazed. "I need to show this to my friend Hammy..."

And off he went to find his friend, carrying the can and the bottle...

Hammy the Squirrel was admiring the meadows when he saw Tico approaching.

"Look what I found," Tico said.

And Hammy said, "You know, you could use it as a telescope..."

They set it up on a tree trunk, and Hammy showed Tico the stars and the Moon.

The local observatory is always well attended as Tico and his friends love to see all the stars and the planets.

A Note from Tico

Hi Everybody:

I hope you liked the story of how Hammy taught us how to watch the Moon and the stars. We have a lot of fun watching the skies on clear nights. I live in the forest, so the skies here are very dark and we can see a lot of different things. We can even see the Milky Way!

Draw pictures of what you see in the sky on the next pages that Deft left blank for you. I'll start you off with a picture of the Moon.

Don't forget to come visit me at www.canyonscientific.net to see what my friends and I are up to. We're still building the site, but you can see how we're doing!

See you in my next adventure,
Tico the Coyote

Color the Moon

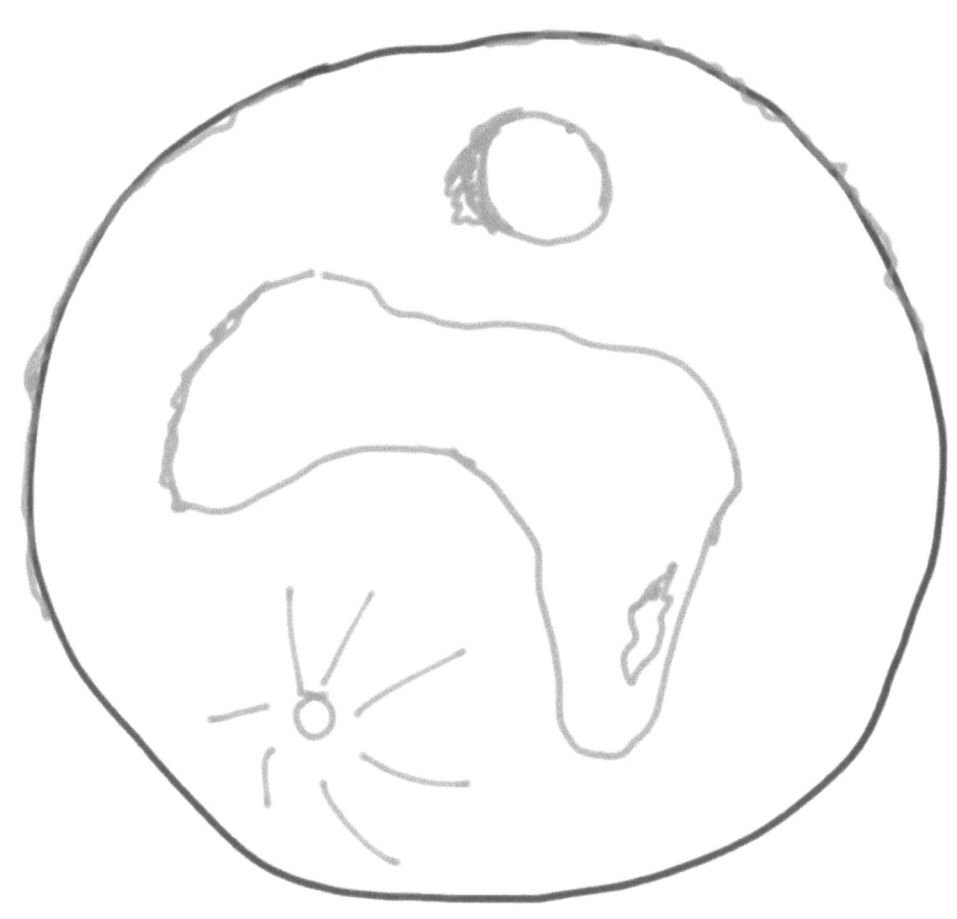

Color the Comet

TAIL
Always points away
from the sun

COMET

SUN
NEVER LOOK
AT THE SUN !

Color the Big Dipper

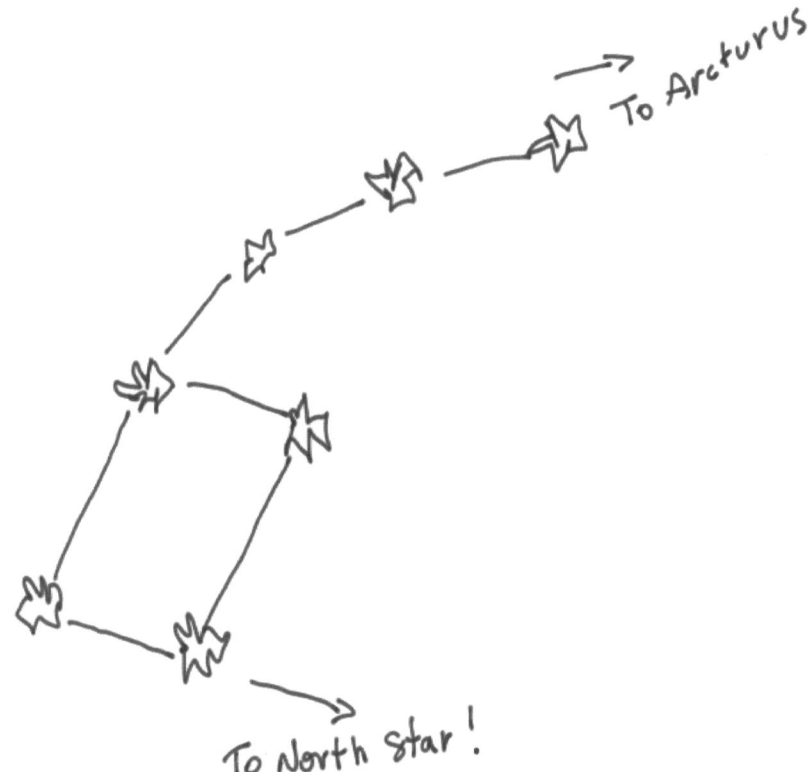

To Arcturus

To North Star!

Connect the Dots

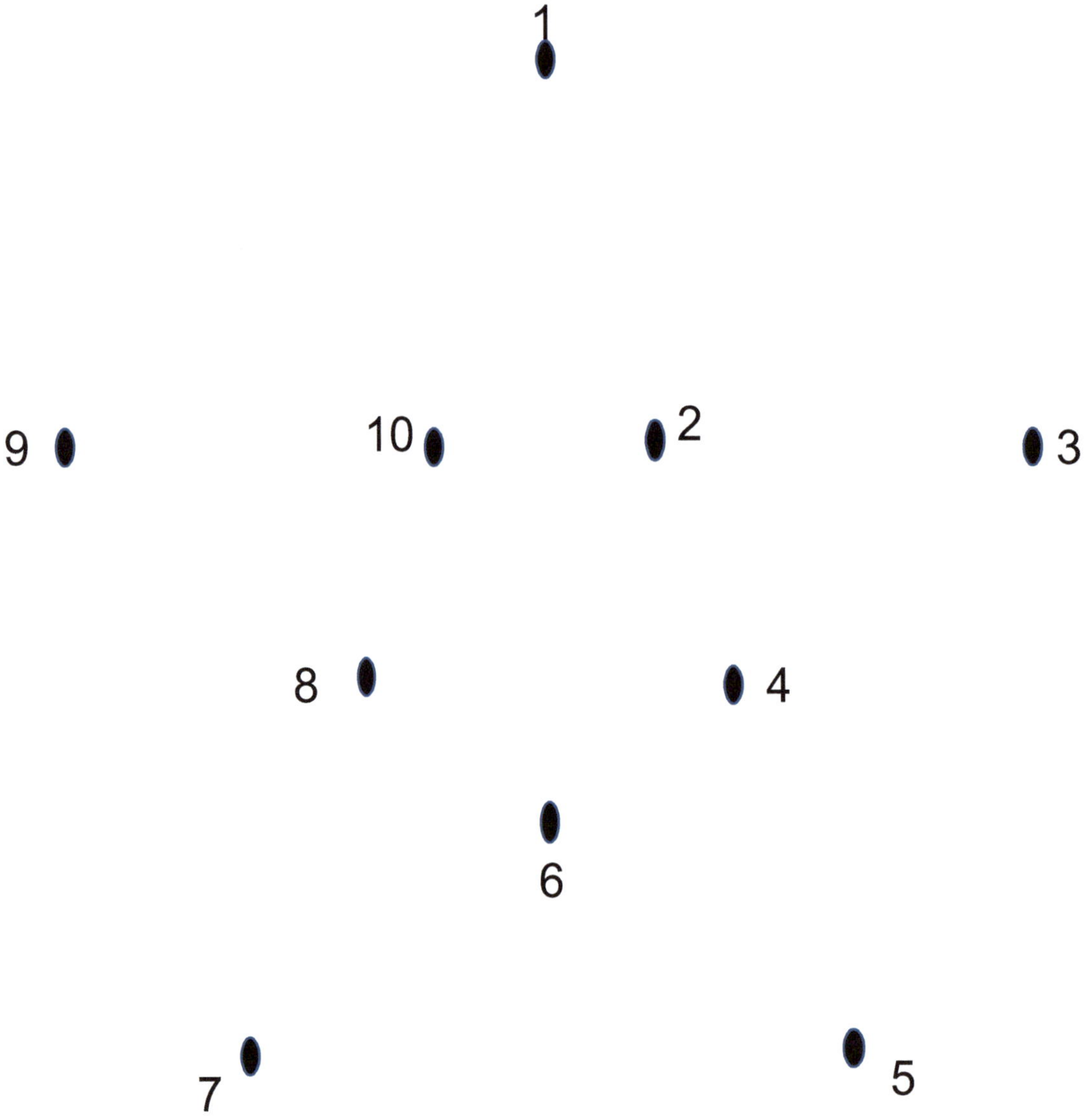

1

10   2

9   3

8   4

6

7   5

18

Draw what you see in the sky.

What else did you see? Draw it here.

Other Tico Stories

Tico Finds a Teddy Bear
Tico Finds a Bicycle